EXTRAORDINARY
WARREN

A SUPER CHICKEN

by Sarah Dillard

ALADDIN

New York   London   Toronto   Sydney   New Delhi

ALADDIN
An imprint of Simon & Schuster Children's Publishing Division
1230 Avenue of the Americas, New York, NY 10020
First Aladdin paper-over-board edition February 2014
Copyright © 2014 by Sarah Dillard
All rights reserved, including the right of reproduction in whole or in part in any form.
ALADDIN is a trademark of Simon & Schuster, Inc., and related logo is a registered trademark of Simon & Schuster, Inc.
For information about special discounts for bulk purchases, please contact Simon & Schuster Special Sales at 1-866-506-1949 or business@simonandschuster.com.
The Simon & Schuster Speakers Bureau can bring authors to your live event. For more information or to book an event contact the Simon & Schuster Speakers Bureau at 1-866-248-3049 or visit our website at www.simonspeakers.com.
Designed by Jeanine Henderson
The text of this book was set in Carnes Handscript and Jacoby.
The illustrations for this book were rendered digitally.
Manufactured in China 1113 SCP
10 9 8 7 6 5 4 3 2 1
This book has been catalogued with the Library of Congress.
ISBN 978-1-4424-5340-1
ISBN 978-1-4424-5341-8 (eBook)

CHAPTER

Once there was a chicken.

Just an ordinary, average,
run-of the-mill chicken.

He lived in a little barnyard
on a quiet farm.

His name was Warren.

Warren was not the only chicken
on the farm. There were lots of others.

They spent their days pecking for chicken feed.
They pecked all day long.

EVERY SINGLE DAY.

It drove Warren . . .

CRAZY.

The chickens stopped pecking.
They looked at one another.
And laughed.

They didn't understand Warren.

He felt very alone.

CHAPTER 2

Warren wasn't the only one who was unhappy.

Millard the rat was also looking for something different.

But day in, day out, all he found was junk.

It made Millard . . .

TRASH.

SUNDAY

RUBBISH.

MONDAY

CRANKY!

At that moment, Warren walked by.

He couldn't believe his ears.

15

As Millard dreamed of better meals to come . . .

Warren rushed home
to share his news.

Warren was as cheerful as he had ever been.
There was just one problem.

CHAPTER 3

When Millard awoke from his nap, he couldn't believe his eyes. Or his luck. A chicken AND an egg.

How extraordinary!

He climbed on top of the trash can, and to his delight, saw even more chickens!

Meanwhile, back at the barnyard, Coach Stanley had big plans for the flock.

Warren heard the whistle and Coach Stanley's announcement.

He got to thinking.

Warren raced to the farm, making
his way to the front of the class.

Coach Stanley made flying look easy.

The chicks lined up to take their turns.

Warren was the last to go.

Warren's hopes
and dreams
were dashed.

He was so
upset he couldn't
even face Egg.

CHAPTER 4

At the trash can, Millard was busy planning himself a feast.

Hey, Little Tender.

Hello, sir.

As Millard left,
Warren noticed
the book he was
carrying.

And then he realized . . .

Sure enough, Warren saw the chickens
were about to walk into trouble . . .

and into Millard.

Warren told the chicks
Millard's REAL plans.

But no one believed him.

They were too excited about the barbecue.

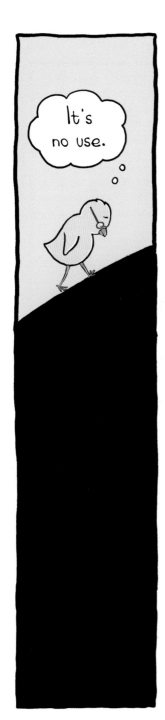

42

CHAPTER 5

Without even thinking, Warren

FLAPPED!

JUMPED!

And flew!

Millard was almost ready for his barbeque.

The table
was set.

The grill was
ready to light.

He was waiting for the main course
to arrive, when all of a sudden . . .

Slowly, Millard sat up.
He was furious when he saw the mess!

My grill is destroyed!

The barbeque is OFF!

As soon as Millard stormed away . . .

the chickens arrived.

CHAPTER

But, not all of the chickens had left.
Warren felt a tap, tap on his back.

He turned around.

The two feathered friends headed home,
walking and talking.

Warren and Egg stopped in their tracks.

And off they went . . .

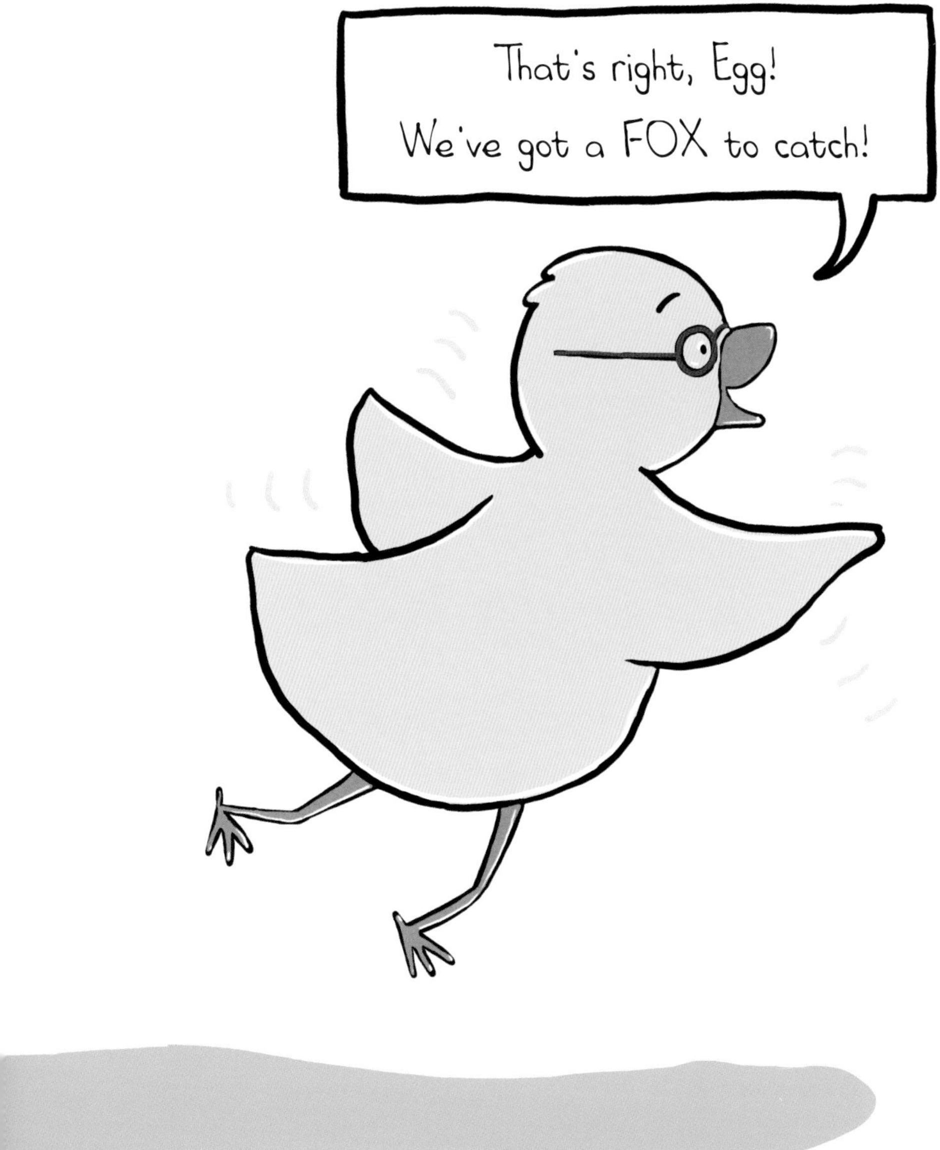
That's right, Egg!
We've got a FOX to catch!

Sarah Dillard grew up in a small town in Massachusetts. She studied art and English literature at Wheaton College, and illustration at the Rhode Island School of Design. She lives on a mountain in Vermont with her husband and dog, both of whom inspire many of her characters, and ensure that she goes for a walk every day. You can visit Sarah online at sarahdillard.com.